Israel Mauduit

Strictures on the Philadelphia Mischianza

Triumph upon Leaving America Unconquered - with extracts, containing

the principal part of a letter

Israel Mauduit

Strictures on the Philadelphia Mischianza
Triumph upon Leaving America Unconquered - with extracts, containing the principal part of a letter

ISBN/EAN: 9783337382377

Printed in Europe, USA, Canada, Australia, Japan

Cover: Foto ©Andreas Hilbeck / pixelio.de

More available books at **www.hansebooks.com**

STRICTURES

ON THE

PHILADELPHIA

MISCHIANZA OR TRIUMPH

UPON LEAVING

America Unconquered.

WITH

EXTRACTS, containing the principal Part of a
LETTER, publifhed in the "*American Crifis*."

In order to fhew how far the King's Enemies think
his General deferving of Public Honours.

N. B. A flattering Account of this Mifchianza was publifhed in the *Philadelphia Gazette*, and copied into the
Morning Poft the 13th of *July* laft; and a larger one by
a ftill more flattering Panegyrift, may be found in the
Gentleman's Magazine for *Auguft* laft.

L O N D O N:

PRINTED FOR J. BEW, PATER-NOSTER-ROW.

M.DCC.LXXIX.

STRICTURES, &c.

IF Sir W——m H—e had thought fit quietly to refign his command, and been content to enjoy in privacy the fortune he had acquired, till the nation had in fome meafure digefted the difgraces and loffes we had fuffered under his command in America; or till the dangers and calamities, which, in confequence of them, threaten us here at home, were paffed over;—he might not then perhaps have been difturbed in his retirement.

But at a time when the Britifh empire in America is funk, and when thou-

fands

fands and thoufands of good fubjects in both countries are ruined by its fall—at a time, when, with the lofs of our Colonies, the empire here in Britain itfelf is fhaken and endangered—at fuch a time of public calamity, when every good Englifhman was trembling for the commonwealth—at fuch a time of diftrefs, for a General to take to himfelf ovations and triumphs greater than the Duke of Marlborough, or any Englifh commander ever thought of—to fuffer himfelf to be crowned with laurels, and to have triumphal arches erected to his honour—is fuch an infult offered to our underftandings, as cannot but raife in the mind of every man of fenfe, the higheft degree of aftonifhment and indignation.

I do not at prefent bring any charge, or enquire *now* where we ought to fix the blame; but this we are fure of, that during the whole of G——l H——'s command, our attempts to fubdue the rebellion have been every where unfuc-

cefsful;

cefsful; the Britifh arms have been continually difgraced, and the Britifh empire in America is loft.

'Tis a Wafhington, therefore, and not
a H—e, that is triumphant. Yet the
Victor General is content to enjoy his
fuccefs in modeft filence ; while the Van-
quifhed, inftead of hiding his head in
obfcurity, moft prepofteroufly covers it
with laurels.

It is no unufual artifice for a Gover-
nor, when leaving his command, to get
his creatures and dependents to fet on
foot an addrefs of thanks : and from a
little Weft India ifland, which none but
its own planters know any thing about,
this may pafs here in England as a proof
of his good behaviour. But could a
Commander in Chief, in a war of fo much
importance—after the nation had been
put to the expence of fo many millions
to no purpofe—and when fo many thoufands of good fubjects are ruined by the
mifcarriage of it—could *he* think, that
we fhould lofe all fenfe of the public

calamities,

calamities, becaufe he expreffes no feel-
ings for them ? Did he think we fhould
imagine that America was ftill ours,
becaufe he fhewed no fhame, but had a
triumph made for him upon the lofs of
it ? Or that a three years feries of perpe-
tual difgraces would not be feen through
all his ovations and triumphal arches ?

How much foever it may be in a General's power to reprefent his army as
greater or lefs, to fuit any prefent occa-
fion, yet one thing at leaft is certain,
that G——l H—e was furnifhed with a
force abundantly fufficient to have quel-
led the rebellion. Both friends and foes
agree in this, that from the year 1776
he never met Mr. Wafhington but with
an army fuperior in *number*, as well as in
goodnefs, to that of the enemy which
was oppofed to him : yet, in the courfe
of three campaigns, he never thought
proper to fight Mr. Wafhington, but
once; and then did not chufe to purfue
the victory which his troops had gained
for him. Either, therefore, the Britifh

troops

troops muſt have been the greateſt of all poltroons, who were unable to contend with an inferior number of new-raiſed, half-clothed, and half-armed American militia ;—or elſe there muſt have been an extreme deficiency in our Generalſhip. Whichſoever of theſe may have been the caſe, what ground can either of them afford for a triumph ? Or upon what foundation could a General—who had ſeen the Britiſh arms endure innumerable diſgraces under his command—who had ſuffered himſelf to be ingloriouſly driven out of Boſton—and who, after having been beaten at Trenton and at Prince-town, was ſtill more ingloriouſly driven out of the Jerſeys—whoſe troops, by bravely beating in the rebel' outpoſts, had often pointed out to him the way to victory, while he never choſe to follow it ; but invariably allowed the Americans to march off unmoleſted, and un-purſued—who had ſuffered himſelf to be ſurpriſed at German-town, and had ſeen his army thereby brought to the brink

of

of deftruction, from which it was refcued
by the fingle bravery and good conduct
of General Mufgrave—who had been
baffled and defeated in all his attempts,
and out-generaled even by a man that
was none—and who now, after three
years command, found himfelf much
lefs able to fupprefs the rebellion, than
he was the day he landed on Staten
Ifland ?—Upon what pretence, I fay,
could this gentleman fuffer himfelf to be
crowned with laurels which he never
won ? Or encourage the *dedicating* a triumphal arch with plumes and military
trophies to his honour, without his having once had the honour of a conqueft ?

A General with fo extenfive and un-
controlled a command, cannot want
flatterers enough among his numerous
dependants, who may have been pro-
moted by his favour, or poffibly enrich-
ed by his connivance.

But when fo very extraordinary a me-
thod has been taken to perfuade us of
the high eftimation in which he is held

for

for his military abilities *, it is a piece of juſtice due to the public, to produce the opinion which the reſt of the Americans entertain of him—ſo very different from that which is here given by his flatterers and dependants.

The very high encomiums upon G—l H—e, which for months together after his appointment were printing in the news-papers, had raiſed in the minds of the Americans the greateſt opinion of his military abilities; and upon the arrival of the troops in 1776, had rendered him an objeɛt of reverence to the King's friends there, and of terror to his enemies. The ſtrong prepoſſeſſions which the Loyaliſts had imbibed in his favour, would not allow them to ſuppoſe that he did not ſee the advantages he then had over the Rebels; and the many opportunities for cruſhing the rebellion, which preſented themſelves in the courſe

* Even on the admiſſion tickets, the General's creſt was encircled with military trophies.

of

of that campaign. They found, however, that he permitted every one of them to pafs away unimproved. If *they* could fee thefe advantages, it could not be fuppofed but that a General of fuch confummate knowledge muft fee much more of them, and know much better than they how to make ufe of them— if he had chofe it. Hence they generally concluded, that he muft have received fecret orders not to hurt the Americans. And with many of them this fufpicion is not eradicated to this day. But whatever may have been their fentiments about the *caufe* of his not conquering, fcarce a man of them had a doubt but that he might have done it.

By the end of the year 1776, this high reputation which the General had brought over with him, was wearing out. Many of the Americans became better informed; and the more difcerning part reflected, that no minifter could have dared to give fuch orders.

The

The inftant they conceived that his conduct proceeded from himfelf, and was the effect of his own choice, and not of orders, they found themfelves at no lofs in forming their judgment. The wretched ufe he had made of his fuppofed fuperiority of Generalfhip, and of his real fuperiority of force, had gradually opened men's eyes, and cured them of all their prejudices in his favour. The friends of government, with indignation, faw that he *did* nothing; and they in charity perhaps might wifh filently to think, what its enemies there openly fay, that he *knew* nothing,

Thefe high encomiums on the General had been the puffs of their own allies here in England; and therefore among the Rebels this deception lafted the longer: but having once got over it, they were the firft to renounce it: and Rebels and Royalifts both at length concurred in the fame opinion. The words of a letter addreffed to him by the former are, *The character of Sir W—m H—e*

has

has undergone some extraordinary revolu-
tions since his arrival in America: it is
now fixed and known; and we have nothing
to hope from your candour, or to fear from
your capacity. The loyal part of the
Americans equally feel this revolution in
their sentiments: and after having seen
the rebel army nine * times succeffively
permitted to go off with impunity, and
unpursued, they would perhaps only
wish to transpose the expreffions, and say
" that they had nothing to hope from
his capacity, and every thing to fear from
what is here called his candour."

Should the reader wish to fee the
grounds of this change of fentiment in
the minds of the American loyalifts, he
will find them in four excellent letters,
figned *Matter of Fact,* printed in the Public Advertifer of the 25th of May, and the
5th, 11th, and 13th of June laft. They
are manifeftly written by a very intelli-
gent eye witnefs, who was prefent with

* See thefe inftances enumerated in the Poftfcript.

the

the army, and acquainted with all its proceedings. They are such as ought to be read by every good Englishman, who wishes to understand the subject; and with a supplemental one in the Morning Post of the 15th of July, are well worth reprinting, now that gentlemen are come to town, who never see the daily papers while they are in the country. If these should not easily be found, the letter signed *Lucius*, in the Morning Chronicle of the 11th of January last, contains many particulars of the same sort.

But as the good opinion of the King's loyal subjects in America seems not to have made a principal object of this gentleman's concern, it may carry more conviction perhaps to produce the opinion which the King's enemies entertain of him; and give the sentiments of the Rebels themselves, who, as the reader will see, acknowledge that through the whole of the campaign of 1776, Mr. H—e's army consisted of nearly double the number

ber of that which Mr. Wafhington oppofed to him—that America was then
young and unfkilled, whereas he was in
high reputation, and his military knowledge was *then* fuppofed to be compleat—
that his troops had arrived in full numbers, and in full fpirits: he was then,
they fay, formidable; and, in effect,
own that he had only to begin to make
an end of them—that their fate was fuf-
pended by a thread—and that, they were
faved as it were, by miracle. After all
thefe acknowledgments of his mercy, the
General might have hoped, that thefe
men, who had been fo often fpared by
him, and conftantly fuffered to withdraw
themfelves, whither they pleafed, from
every dangerous fituation, would at leaft
have treated him with refpect. But as
men who have broke through their
oaths, and caft off their allegiance, naturally throw away with it their grati-
tude, and every other fenfe of obligation,
the return which they make to the General, who they in effect acknowledge
might

might fo often have cruſhed them, is to treat him with every kind of indignity; and to ſpeak of him in terms of the ut-moſt ſcorn and contempt.

The *American Criſis* is a work which has been publiſhed in numbers; and has come out upon particular occaſions, when the Congreſs has judged it neceſſary to rouze and animate their adherents in their reſiſtance againſt this country. It profeſſes to be written by the author of *Common Senſe*. Some have given it to Dr. Franklin, others to Mr. Adams.

It is now known to be written under the patronage of the Congreſs, and the inſtructions of their capital and beſt in-formed leaders.

The fifth number was publiſhed in March laſt, when the Congreſs were in expectation of ſome conciliatory offers being brought to them from Great Bri-tain; and were apprehenſive that their people might be weary of the war, and induced to accept them.

The

The arguments ufed to prevent this are, " That although at firft the Britifh arms were formidable, and G——l H—e might then have eafily fubdued them, yet now they have found him out :—That they had nothing to fear from his ca-pacity; and that Mr. Wafhington has conftantly out-generaled him:—That if in the year 1776, when he was in his ftrongeft ftate, and they in their weakeft, he did not then take the way to conquer, they had nothing to fear from him now, when their force was greater, and when his was rather lefs, and his credit with them none at all.

" That by giving them three years training, he had taught them their bu-finefs; and they were now able to meet their enemy upon any ground; and therefore had no need to treat."

This firft part is called, *A Letter to General Sir W——m H—e.* The other two parts are, *An Addrefs to the Americans;* and *A Plan for maintaining a*
Standing

Standing Army, superior to any Force which shall be brought against them. Great part of the book is too full of the most virulent invective against the King, the Parliament, and the English nation, to bear re-printing; but will abundantly satisfy the reader, that it can be the work of no one but a most strenuous advocate for American Independence, and a man full of the most rancorous malice against this country.

A confederate here in England, if he please, may reprint the whole book, containing thirty-two pages. I shall only give some extracts from the first part of it, to shew the opinion which our enemies have of the General's conduct, and how little they must think him deserving of this public triumph.

The title is :

" THE

"THE

"AMERICAN CRISIS,

"NUMBER V.

"ADDRESSED TO

" General Sir W————M H——E.

" By the Author of COMMON SENSE.

" LANCASTER, Printed;

" HARTFORD, Re-printed;

" And fold by WATSON and GOODWIN, near the
" Great Bridge. 1778."

The reader will make the proper allowance for the boafts of party; and will obferve, that the author continually gives his leaders the credit of after-wifdom and after-defign, which they never had the leaft thought of before the events.

It

It fets out with fome affected wit and ill-judged abufe; and then after fome more perfonal charges, the letter goes on :

" That a man, whofe foul is abforbed
" in the low traffic of vulgar vice, is in-
" capable of moving in any fuperior re-
" gion, is clearly fhown in you by the
" event of every campaign;—your mili-
" tary exploits have been without plan,
" object, or decifion. Can it be poffible
" that you or your employers can fup-
" pofe the poffeffion of Philadelphia to
" be any ways equal to the expence or
" expectation of the nation which fup-
" ports you ?   What advantages does
" England derive from any atchive-
" ments of yours ? To her it is perfectly
" indifferent what place you are in, fo
" long as the bufinefs of conqueft is un-
" performed, and the charge of main-
" taining you remains the fame.

" If the principal events of the three

C   " campaigns

" campaigns be attended to, the balance
" will appear ftrongly againft you at the
" clofe of each ; but the laft, in point of
" importance to us, hath exceeded the
" former two. It is pleafant to look
" back on dangers paft, and equally as
" pleafant to meditate on prefent ones,
" when the way out begins to appear.
" That period is now arrived, and the
" long doubtful winter of war is changed
" to the fweeter profpects of victory and
" joy. At the clofe of the campaign in
" feventy-five, you were obliged to re-
" treat from Bofton. In the fummer,
" feventy-fix, you appeared with a nu-
" merous fleet and army in the harbour
" of New York. *By what miracle the*
" *Continent was preferved in that feafon of*
" *danger is a fubject of admiration.* If,
" inftead of wafting your time againft
" Long Ifland, you had run up the
" North River, and landed any where
" above New York, the confequence
" muft have been, that either you would
" have compelled General Wafhington

" to

" to fight you with very unequal num-
" bers, or he muft have fuddenly evacu-
" ated the city, with the lofs of nearly
" all the ftores of the army, or have fur-
" rendered for want of provifions ; the
" fituation of the place naturally pro-
" ducing one or other of thefe events*.

* The map will convince the reader of the juft-
nefs of this obfervation ; and both friends and enemies at the time concurred in making it. For weeks
together, after the General had fuffered the rebels to
efcape from Long Ifland, where the loyal part of the
Americans expected day after day, that he would
land at New Rochelle, and march to the north river, while his fleet failed up it. All men faw (and
fome, it has been publickly faid, told him) that he
would thereby fhut up the rebel army in the penin-
fula of New York ; and were wondering and la-
menting that he did not inftantly do it, and thereby
retrieve the falfe ftep he had made. Yet the General
lay quiet in his camp at New-town for above a fort-
night, while his enemies were recovering from their
terror. And many of his officers, it is faid, with their
glaffes, faw them carry off cannon and ftores from
New York crofs the eaft river, to guard as well as
they could againft the danger.

" The

" The preparations made to defend
" New York were, neverthelefs, wife
" and military; becaufe your forces were
" then at fea, their numbers uncertain;
" ftorms, ficknefs, or a variety of acci-
" dents might have difabled their com-
" ing, or fo diminifhed them on their
" paffage, that thofe which furvived
" would have been incapable of the
" campaign with any profpect of fuccefs;
" in which cafe the defence would have
" been fufficient, and the place pre-
" ferved : for cities that have been raifed
" from nothing with an infinitude of
" labour and expence, are not to be
" thrown away on any probability of
" their being taken. On thefe grounds
" the preparations made to maintain
" New York were as judicious as the
" retreat afterwards. *While you in the*
" *interim let flip the very* OPPORTUNITY
" *which feemed to put conqueft in your power.*

" Through the whole of that cam-
" paign *you had nearly double the forces*
" *which*

" *which General Washington immediately*
" *commanded.* The principal plan at
" that time on our part, was to wear
" away the feafon with as little lofs as
" poffible, and to raife the army for the
" next year. Long Ifland, New York,
" Forts Wafhington and Lee, were not
" defended (after your fuperior force was
" known) under any expectation of their
" being finally maintained, but as a
" range of out-works, in the attacking
" of which your time might be wafted,
" your numbers reduced, and your va-
" nity amufed, by poffeffing them on
" our retreat. It was intended to have
" withdrawn the garrifon from Fort
" Wafhington, after it had anfwered
" the former of thefe purpofes; but the
" fate of that day put a prize into your
" hands, without much honour to your-
" felves,

" Your progrefs through the Jerfeys
" was accidental: you had it not even
" in contemplation, or you would not

C 3 " have

" have fent fo principal a part of your
" force to Rhode Ifland before hand.
" The utmoft hope of America, in the
" year feventy-fix, reached no higher
" than that fhe might not *then* be con-
" quered, She had no expectation of
" defeating you in the campaign. Even
" the moft cowardly Tory allowed, that
" could fhe withftand the fhock of that
" Summer, her independence would be
" paft a doubt. You had then greatly
" the advantage of her; you were for-
" midable; your military knowledge
" was *fuppofed to be compleat; your fleets*
" *and forces arrived without any accident;*
" *you had nothing to do but to begin, and*
" *your chance lay in the firft vigorous onfet.*

" America was young and unfkilled.
" She was obliged to truft her defence to
" time and practice; and hath, by mere
" dint of perfeverance, maintained her
" caufe, and brought her enemy to a
" condition in which fhe is now capable
" of meeting him on any ground.

" It

" It is remarkable, that in the cam-
" paign of seventy-six, you gained no
" more, notwithstanding your great
" force, than what was given you by
" consent or evacuation, except Fort
" Washington; while every advantage
" obtained by us was by fair and hard
" fighting. The defeat of Sir Peter
" Parker was complete. The conquest
" of the Hessians by the remains of a
" retreating army, which but a few days
" before you affected to despise*, is an
" instance of heroic perseverance very
" seldom to be met with; and the vic-
" tory

---

* It did not suit this author's argument to say,
whom you mercifully spared; though, in the House
of Commons, the General valued himself upon his
mercy. And it will be hard to find in history so
striking an instance. The words of the gazette are:
" *All these motions plainly indicating the enemy's design
to avoid coming to action, I did not think the driving
their rear guard further back an object of the least con-
sequence.*" That is, " finding them now the fifth time

disposed

" tory over the Britiſh troops at Prince
" town, by a harraſſed and weary party,
" who had been engaged the day before,
" and marched all night without re-
" freſhment, is attended with ſuch a
" ſcene of circumſtances, and ſuperiority
" of Generalſhip, as will ever give it a
" place on the firſt line in the hiſtory of
" great actions.

" When I look back on the gloomy
" days of laſt winter, *and ſee America*
" *ſuſpended by a thread*, I feel a triumph
" of joy at the recollection of her de-

diſpoſed to go off without fighting, I did not think
it of the leaſt conſequence to prevent them; but permitted them to ſcramble over the north river as they
could—to fly a hundred miles over the Jerſeys half
purſued, and then to croſs the Delaware, and get to
Philadelphia, without any moleſtation."

In all other wars, a General's finding that his enemy wiſhed to go off without fighting, has been
thought a reaſon for preſſing him ſo much the more:
In the American war it is given as a reaſon for not
preſſing him at all.

" livery,

" livery, and a reverence for the cha-
" racters which fnatched her from de-
" ftruction, To doubt now would be a
" fpecies of infidelity ; and to forget the
" inftruments which faved us then,
" would be ingratitude.

*　　*　　*　　*

*　　*　　*　　*

" Let me afk, Sir, what great ex-
" ploits have you performed ? Through
" all the variety of changes and oppor-
" tunities, which this war hath pro-
" duced, I know of no one action of
" yours that can be ftiled mafterly. You
" have moved in and out, backward and
" forward, round and round, as if valor
" confifted in a military jig. The hif-
" tory and figure of your movements
" would be truly ridiculous, could they
" be juftly delineated. They refemble
" the labours of a puppy purfuing his
" tail; the end is ftill at the fame dif-
" tance

" tance, and all the turnings round muſt
" be done over again *.

" There has been ſomething unmili-
" tarily paſſive in you, from the time of
" your paſſing the Schuylkill, and get-
" ting poſſeſſion of Philadelphia, to the
" cloſe of the campaign. You miſtook
" a trap for a conqueſt; the probabi-
" lity of which had been made known
" to Europe, and the edge of your
" triumph taken off by our own infor-
" mation long before.

" Having got you into this ſituation,
" a ſcheme for a general attack upon

* I do not adopt this language of contempt; but
if his panegyriſt had not told us, could it have been
thought poſſible, that this gentleman, a month after
this publication, ſhould have had a fame ſpangled
with ſtars, ſtuck upon the top of his triumphal arch,
blowing from her trumpet in letters of light : " Tes
" lauriers ſont immortels." And not content with
this earth's being filled with the ſound of his fame,
ſhe was even powdered with ſtars, to tell us that it
reaches up to the heavens.

" you

" you at German-town was carried into
" execution on the Fourth of October;
" and though the fuccefs was not equal
" to the excellence of the plan, yet the
" attempting it proved the genius of
" America to be on the rife, and her
" power approaching to fuperiority.
" The obfcurity of the morning was
" your beft friend; for a fog is always
" favourable to a hunted enemy. Some
" weeks after this you likewife planned
" an attack on General Wafhington,
" while at Whitemarfh; marched out
" with infinite parade; but on finding
" him preparing to attack you, the next
" morning you prudently cut about,
" and retreated to Philadelphia with all
" the precipitation of a man conquered
" in imagination.

" Immediately after the battle of Ger-
" man-town, the probability of Bur-
" goyne's defeat gave a new policy to
" affairs in Penfylvania; and it was
5   " judged

" judged moft confiftent with the general
" fafety of America to wait the iffue of
" the northern campaign. Slow and
" fure is found work. The news of
" that victory arrived in our camp on
" the 18th of October, and no fooner
" did the fhout of joy, and the report of
" the thirteen cannon reach your ears,
" than you refolved upon a retreat, and
" the next day, that is on the 19th,
" withdrew your drooping army in Phi-
" ladelphia. This movement was evi-
" dently dictated by fear, and carried
" with it a pofitive confeffion, that you
" dreaded a fecond attack. It was hid-
" ing yourfelf among women * and chil-

* Should the reader afk, what it was that the General at laft did among them? his panegyrift has
here told us, " He bounced off with his bombs and
burning hearts, fet upon the pillars of his triumphal
arch, which, at the proper time of the fhow, burft out
in a fhower of fquibs and crackers, and other fire-
works, to the delectable amazement of Mifs Craig,
Mifs Chew, Mifs Redman, and all the other miffes,
dreffed out as the fair damfels of the blended rofe,
and of the burning mountain, for this farce of
knight-errantry."

                                    " dren

" dren, and fleeping away the choiceft
" part of a campaign in expenfive inac-
" tivity. An army in a city can never
" be a conquering army. The fituation
" admits only of defence, It is mere
" fhelter; and every military power in
" Europe will conclude you to be even-
" tually defeated.

" The time when you made this re-
" treat, was the very time you ought to
" have fought a battle, in order to put
" yourfelf in a condition of recovering
" in Penfylvania what you had loft at
" Sarratoga; and the reafon why you
" did not, muft be either prudence or
" c——e; the former fuppofes your
" inability, and the latter needs no ex-
" planation. I draw no conclufions,
" Sir, but fuch as are naturally deduced
" from known or vifible facts, and fuch
" as will always have a being while the
" facts which produced them remain un-
" altered."
   " Lancafter,
     " March 28, 1778."

Such are the fentiments which the Americans entertain of this gentleman, and fo great is the contempt they exprefs of him. It might have been thought impoffible, but the General has hit upon the fingle means of increafing it; and that was by this ill-timed and prepofte- rous medley of a triumph. His ene- mies, we fee, charge him with fleeping away the beft part of the campaign : his friends perhaps may wifh, that all this raree fhow had paffed only in a dream : for no man, they may judge, in his waking thoughts, ought ever to have admitted it.

What would not have been faid of the duke of Marlborough's vanity, if, after forty thoufand enemies killed and taken at the battle of Blenheim, he had en- couraged his officers and dependents to dedicate to him a triumphal arch, and had employed even the *enemies* ftandards taken in battle, in forming an avenue for himfelf and his fellow conquerors to have walked through ?

What

What then are we to think of a beaten General's debafing the King's enfigns (for he had none of his enemies) by planting all the colours of the army in a grand avenue of three hundred feet in length, lined with the King's troops, between two triumphal arches, for himfelf and his brother to march along in pompous proceffion,[1] followed by a numerous train of attendants, with feven filken knights of the blended rofe, and feven more of the burning mountain, and their fourteen Turkey dreffed damfels, to an area of 150 yards fquare, lined alfo with the King's troops, for the exhibition of a tilt and tournament, or mock fight of old chivalry, in honour of this triumphant hero *; and all this fea and land-

* See a lift of the feven knights of the blended rofe, all armed in filk and taffity, who fo defperately maintained in combat the wit and beauty of their fair damfels, againft the feven terrible knights of the burning mountain, fighting in honour of theirs; with the colours and trappings of the horfes, and the mottos and devices, and names, and colours of the riders.

ovation

ovation made—not in confequence of an uninterrupted fucceffion of victories, like thofe of the duke of Marlborough— not after the conqueft of Canada by a Wolfe, a Townfhend, and an Amherft; or after the much more valuable con- queft of all the French provinces and poffeffions in India, under the *wife and active* general Coote—but after thirteen provinces wretchedly loft, and a three years feries of ruinous difgraces and de- feats.

POSTSCRIPT.

IT is faid that the Rebel army has nine times fucceffively been permitted to go off unpurfued.

They who were prefent, and knew the country reckon up more than nineteen opportunities loft, in which the Rebel army might have been deftroyed; but I am led to that number by a letter in a morning paper of the 11th of December laft, which particularizes fo many inftances of the fame fort.

In the attack of trenches the troops behind them fuffer little in the beginning of the action; and the principal lofs falls upon the affailants, while they are marching up to them : but this lofs is amply compenfated by the much greater deftruction of the enemy in the rout and purfuit, after the trenches are

D   forced.

forced. General H—e, who values himfelf upon his mercy, has fome times
over ruled this difpofition fo far as to
order the King's troops upon the *lofing
part* of the attack, in forcing their way
up to the enemies trenches ; but never
had cruelty enough to fuffer the Rebels
to be expofed to the rout and purfuit,
upon their being driven out of them.

If this had happened once or twice
only we might have imputed it to accident :—had it been fuffered three or four
times, we might have fufpected and la-
mented fome failure in the military ca-
pacity :—but when we have feen the fame
thing happen, and the fame manoeuvres
practifed nine times over—when, in the
courfe of three years, the royal army has
never once been permitted to rout and
purfue—it muft require a great extent of
charity indeed to make us impute this
either to accident or incapacity.

The

The LETTER is as follows::

" Friday 11 Dec. 1778.

" Mr. EDITOR,

" IN your account of the debate on
" Friday laft, I fee that Sir W——m
" H—e expreffes a defire that an enquiry
" fhould take place, not only for the fa-
" tisfaction of the houfe, but of the na-
" tion at large. It will greatly contribute
" to the nation's fatisfaction, if he will
" be fo good as to explain to us a
" very remarkable circumftance in the
" conduct of the American war, which
" never has been known in any other.

" In every one of the fuccefsful at-
" tacks which our troops, with fo much
" bravery have made upon their enemy,
" they have always been kept back from
" purfuing, and never once been per-
" mitted to improve the advantages they
" might have gained.

" At

" At Bunker's Hill, the rebels only re-
" treat was over a narrow caufeway; and
" had they been purfued, as General
" Clinton is faid to have advifed, num-
" bers of them muft have been deftroyed,
" or taken.—But this was one of the
" leaft of the errors of that day,

" At Long Ifland, the troops very fuc-
" cefsfully fought their way up to the
" rebel camp, and expreffed the utmoft
" eagernefs to ftorm it, when the Gene-
" ral fent repeated orders for them to de-
" fift from the attempt; although he
" himfelf was of opinion, that it would
" have fucceeded. Even when the whole
" column of the troops was come up,
" they were reftrained for three days from
" forcing the rebel camp, though Mr.
" Wafhington *, and his whole army
" muft

* By the General's telling us that Putnam commanded in the lines, we might be led to fuppofe that
Wafhington was not there. But it was well known
that he was prefent all the time; and after three
days,

" muſt have been taken, or deſtroyed in
" conſequence of it.

" After the rebels had been ſuffered to
" eſcape to New York, inſtead of in-
" ſtantly purſuing them in that ſtate of
" trepidation they were then in, the ar-
" my lay quiet in their camp in Long
" Iſland for ſixteen days, till the rebels
" had time to recover themſelves from
" their fright, and prepare for their de-
" fence.

" When at length the army landed in
" the iſland of New York, the Ameri-
" cans almoſt all of them made their
" eſcape, without being purſued.

" At Kingſbridge, the Gazette tells
" us, they quitted their poſition *with*
" *ſome precipitation*, although without any
" one's purſuing them.

days, when the boats were paſſing backward and
forward all night long in carrying the army over the
ferry, he went off in one of the laſt.

" At

" At the White Plains, the troops, in
" defiance of the enemy's fire, marched
" through the river, poffeffed themfelves
" of one hill, and attacked   routed
" the enemy on another; *and rufhing on*
" *them drove them from their works*; which
" the Gazette fays, *were very material*
" *pofts; and the Heffian grenadiers advanced*
" *to the heights within cannon fhot of the*
" *entrenchments*; yet, far from improv-
" ing thefe advantages, the reft of the
" army, we are told, *did not move*, but
" remained in their camp for four days
" together, till at length the rebels, *hav-*
" *ing intelligence by a deferter of their dan-*
" *ger, moft prudently evacuated their camp.*

    " They left, we are told, a ftrong rear
" guard, at only a mile's diftance; *but*
" *the driving them farther back was not*
" *thought an object of the leaft confequence.*
" Yet General Lee, while he was a pri-
" foner at New York, is faid to have
" often acknowledged, that if the Ame-
" ricans had been attacked in their camp,

       " or

" or purfued after their retreat, their
" army muft have been totally ruined.

" After their running out of Fort
" Lee, when the Rebels were flying acrofs
" the Jerfeys, and Lord Cornwallis was
" in clofe purfuit of them, and might by
" himfelf alone have had the honour of
" deftroying them, he was ftopped fhort
" in his purfuit *(by orders not to advance*
" *beyond Brunfwick)* till the General him-
" felf came up. He did come up, at
" his own leifure, five days after; and
" thereby gave the enemy five days re-
" fpite to efcape over the Delaware at
" theirs.

" The Americans, on the other hand,
" did not neglect to improve the fingle
" advantage they gained at Trenton;
" but pufhed on, and drove the King's
" troops out of Prince Town, the very
" place where that day month Lord
" Cornwallis might have overtaken and
" deftroyed them, if the General had

9
" not

" not ſtopped him in his purſuit. But
" I wiſh to draw a veil over the ſhame-
" ful manner in which we were driven
" out of the Jerſeys.

" During all the time of General
" H—'s command, he has choſen to
" give the enemy battle but once, and
" that was at Brandywine. Yet there
" too, after the troops had gained the
" victory, and Waſhington and his ar-
" my, in the utmoſt confuſion, were
" fled to Philadelphia—there was no
" purſuit, and the army remained inac-
" tive for five days together, till the Re-
" bels ſhould have recovered from their
" conſternation, and ſent off their can-
" non and ſtores; yet a well known let-
" ter from a French officer ſerving a-
" mong them, ſays, that they might then
" alſo have been ruined.

" At German Town, the General, far
" from ſeeking to give battle to the ene-
" my, ſuffered himſelf to be ſurpriſed,

2   " and

" and might have loft his army, if Co-
" lonel Mufgrave had not thrown him-
" felf into a ftrong ftone houfe, and, by
" refolutely defending it, given time to
" the troops to recover themfelves. After
" this they eafily defeated their enemy,
" but were not permitted to purfue,
" which the fame French officer writes
" muft have been fatal to them.

" In fhort, during the whole courfe
" of the war, the General has fought
" juft enough to fecure good winter quar-
" ters at New York and Philadelphia—
" has often made his troops force their
" way up to the enemy, but then they
" have invariably been kept back, and
" never fuffered to improve the advan-
" tages they had gained.

" I leave your readers to make their
" own reflections, but fuch are the facts.

" Had the General made ufe of any
" one of the opportunities, which offer-
E   " ed

" ed in the year 1776, for inclofing and
" cutting off the whole rebel army, I
" do not fay, as many do, that he would
" have made an end of the war too foon;
" but this I fay, and all the Americans,
" Rebels as well as Royalifts, agree in
" this, that he would foon have made
" an end of the war.

CATO·"

FINIS.

www.ingramcontent.com/pod-product-compliance
Lightning Source LLC
Chambersburg PA
CBHW030910260626
47169CB00008B/2778